فيزول عني الخوف.

and I am not afraid anymore.

وتقبلني. . .

and a kiss. . .

تعانقني أمي. . .

Mommy gives me a hug. . .

"رأيت حِلمًا
مزعجًا."

"I had a
bad dream."

"ما الخطب يا
عزيزي؟"

"What's wrong,
honey?"

عندما أشعر بالخوف. . .
أنادي أمي أو أبي.

When I get scared,
I call Mommy or Daddy.

عندما يشعر كلبي بالخوف. . .
يختبئ خلفي.

When my dog is afraid. . .
he hides behind me.

عندما تشعر قطتي بالخوف. . .
تختبئ تحت سريري.

When my kitten is afraid. . .
she hides under my bed.

عندما يشعر الفأر بالخوف. . . .
يهرع إلى داخل حفرة.

When a mouse is afraid. . .
it hurries into a hole.

عندما يشعر السنجاب بالخوف. . .
يفر متسلقًا أعلى الشجرة.

When a squirrel is afraid. . .
it scampers up a tree.

عندما تشعر السلحفاة بالخوف. . .
تنكمش على نفسها داخل درقتها .

When a turtle is afraid. . .
it shrinks into its shell.

عندما يشعر أرنب بالخوف. . .
يهرع إلى داخل الشجيرات

When a rabbit is afraid. . .
it races into the bushes.

عندما يشعر الغراب بالخوف. . .
يطير بعيدًا.

When crows are afraid. . .
they fly away.

عندما تشعر الضفادع بالخوف. . .
تغطس في بركة ماء.

When frogs are afraid. . .
they dive into a pond.

عندما يشعر السمك بالخوف. . . .
يندفع بسرعة بعيدًا.

When fish are afraid. . .
they dart away.

عندما تشعر الزرافة بالخوف. . .
تهرب بسرعة قدر الإمكان.

When a giraffe is afraid. . .
it runs away as fast as it can.

عندما تشعر النعامة بالخوف. . .
تدفن رأسها في الرمال.

When an ostrich is afraid. . .
it buries its head in the sand.

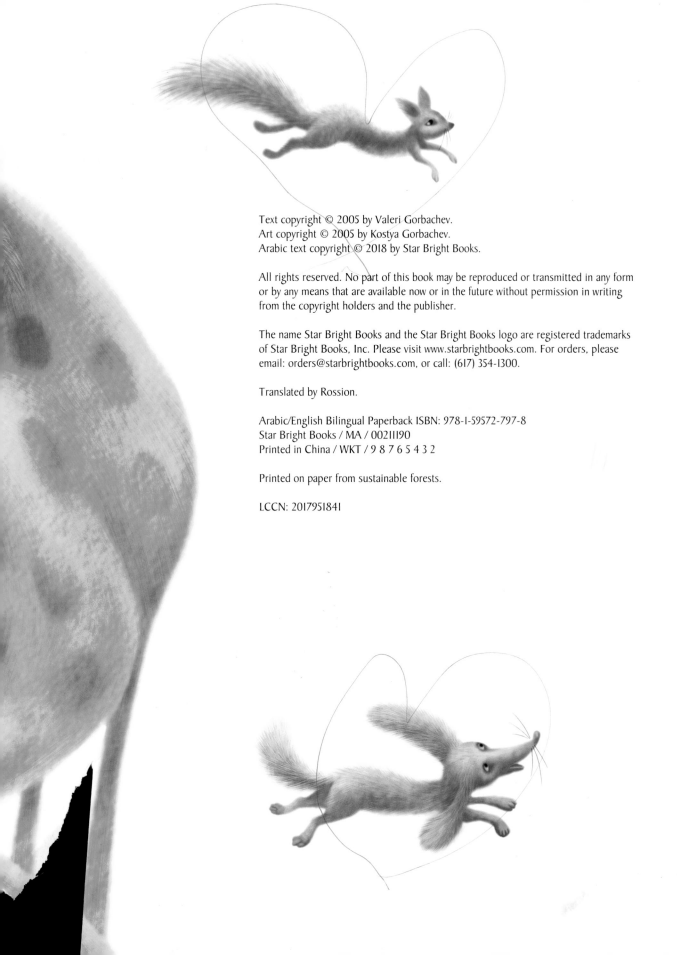

Translated by Rossion.

Arabic/English Bilingual Paperback ISBN: 978-1-59572-797-8
Star Bright Books / MA / 00211190
Printed in China / WKT / 9 8 7 6 5 4 3 2

Printed on paper from sustainable forests.

LCCN: 2017951841

عندما يشعر
أحدهم بالخوف

When Someone is Afraid

By Valeri Gorbachev بقلم فاليري غورباتشاف
Illustrated by Kostya Gorbachev أعد الرسوم كوستيا غورباتشاف

STAR BRIGHT BOOKS
CAMBRIDGE MASSACHUSETTS